RYKAR

TALES OF DUREIZEN

ALSO BY ZAVEN BOSWELL

THE SHADOW BLOOD TALE

FESTER

TALES OF DUREIZEN

RYKAR

RYKAR

— 1 —

TALES OF DUREIZEN

ZAVEN BOSWELL

I wash away the remainder of the man's blood from my claws. They may become bloody again tomorrow, but at least this way I can appreciate their temporary splendor. Shiny, murderous, swift, and beautiful. Without them, my hands would become soiled in sin. This way, my devices killed the man, not I.

Once the last bit of blood is cleaned from my blades, I set them down, then I begin to fill each of the glass jars next to me with fresh, cold water. First, the one containing the heart, then the lungs, liver, pancreas, and lastly, the brain. Every one of these will be given to someone who can utilize their potential in some way—perhaps simply observing their complexities or attempting to revive the dead. Either way, they are useless to me: useless like being trapped inside their previous owner.

He was coughing up a storm before I even let him inside.

And even though both of us understood his harsh reality, I believe every human deserves a fighting chance. Still, it was obvious this man wasn't going to live another week. Poor fellow. Lung cancer is a terrible affliction. Like him, people from all over the continent of Windsor come to me in hopes their deadly diseases can be cured, but they are mistaken. I'm a doctor, yes, but I know my limits. I will cure what is fixable. Others will meet a less painful death and be used for a greater purpose other than rotting away for another day on this planet.

I seal the lid on the final jar containing the brain. The body has already been disposed of, resting outside to be transported away. Now to hand over the rest of him.

The jars clink together as I hug them. One single trip, for the courier has been waiting long enough.

Once I open my door to head outside, the familiar figure stands before me, preventing me from exiting my home. He does this all the time. I'm aware that under his bird mask lies an unemotional face of stone, and within those black robes rests a knife as assurance to obtain the requested goods. Daunting, but I'm numb to the feeling. If only I could've cured him, then Birdman would have no purpose being here. Just a hassle I must deal with every morning.

he figure shifts and bends to my level as I pass him every jar at once, his movements attentive to prevent anything from falling and shattering. Would he kill me if such a thing occurred? The goods would become soiled, so perhaps. Still, I enjoy this risk. I'm sick of most days involving killing over curing.

He succeeds in acquiring the man's organs. I'm left empty-handed.

With a singular nod, he leaves. Once his back is turned, my eyes follow his every movement like prey, observing any possible internal struggles that may mark him as a future target. I struggle to see anything amiss as he leisurely places the jars into the wagon containing my patient. Afterward, he hoists himself onto the front seat and departs, his black steed trotting away to Gresiden.

It's typical of him to not spare me another glance. One day, he may be my next patient, and if he's incurable, I'll bring his body back to Gresiden myself. Not like he would risk such a thing anyway. Besides, there are worse people to collaborate with. At least he always pays me a large sum prior to handing him the goods. The hassle of confirming everything's in order before payment would be insufferable.

I inhale and let the fresh, cool air freeze every cavity of my lungs. Soon it shall be winter. At this moment, the northern kingdoms must already be making preparations, and so should I. Countless people with varying degrees of frostbite will enter my home next month, wishing for me to cure the harsh weather's affliction alongside their primary issue that warranted the trip. I really should give up on them. Those cases always end in failure.

At least this profession has given me enough popularity and revenue to live comfortably. Sure, there are times when officials from Gresiden visit me, questioning the disappearances of others, but they are weak-minded creatures. Simple answers are all I need. 'She left when I cured her, unsure where she went.' 'I couldn't save him; his body has already been sent away.' 'I cannot recall anybody by that name.' If they dare to linger and watch me work, then I turn those away who I cannot help.

Furthermore, the distance between my home and that oversized town discourages the trek. People detest traveling all this way solely based on false suspicions. People prefer to visit only when they have something to gain. My reputation speaks for itself, saving humans who believed they had a terminal disease, only for it to be a nasty, treatable flu. Survivors will spread tales. The dead will stay silent.

I slam the door behind me and return to my claws. A few of the blades possess nicks and scratches despite how much I tend to them, but there's nothing I can do to prevent time's curse. Everything decays. I just wish to live long enough to discover some purpose for my existence. What I do is meaningful, but witnessing constant suffering is dreadful. No. This can't be all I'm meant for.

Movement outside the window captures my attention. A slim figure, heading in my direction, walks opposite of the wagon's course. She holds herself with incredible poise. Her long, brown hair rests carefully on her shoulders. Her deep, green eyes shine bright as the sunlight. Her curves proclaim how healthy she is without worry of malnutrition or sickness. A true light in the darkness.

Could she have walked all this way? Many people prefer to pay another for ease of travel, especially when feeling unwell. Some even go as far as tracking down my courier to ride here in the morning. Few choose to walk all this way, an option left for those without coin. However, she appears to be wealthy enough, so why does she insist on not having proper transport?

I must make myself presentable, for who knows what she desires from me. Surely, she cannot be a client, but why else would she care to meet someone like me?

I rush into my office and set my claws on the workbench next to the vast variety of books and medicinal flowers. Once my hands can no longer sense their warm, soft texture, I head toward the water basin and mirror on the opposite side of the room. When I arrive, I look behind my shoulders to confirm if the claws are still where I left them and that my shadow hasn't stolen them or wished for me to keep them on. Nothing. So, I turn around and stare into the mirror.

Green eyes just like her. I guess mine fail to shine with such brilliance. As for my skin, small wrinkles around the eyes and mouth flaunt telltale signs of age. It feels ragged and appears dull despite me just turning thirty not long ago. Additionally, my black hair is tangled like an abandoned bird's nest, obviously due to my endeavor this morning. Doing great things requires total concentration not on oneself. Besides, hair can always be readjusted.

I dunk my hands into the water, then move them above my hair. Here, I let the liquid slide down my fingers, allowing it to drip onto the patches that are too messy for comfort. The remainder sticking to my skin helps mold the awkward strands into something more presentable. My hair is always messy, but too much would deem unprofessional, too little would deem too sophisticated. The ones who can cure tragedies must appear abnormal.

A light series of knocks echoing into my office indicates I am out of time. I dry my hands on my clothes as I rush to the door. Opening it, the woman from my window stands before me, even more beautiful and animate up close.

"To who do I owe this pleasure?" I ask, confident in my greeting.

The woman's eyes glance over my entire appearance. Judgmental, but what is she trying to discern?

"Are you Rykar?" she asks. Even her voice is like

angels speaking down on mere mortals.

"I am. To who do I owe this pleasure?" I emphasize again. I need to know her name. Why is she here?

"Isabelle. For someone who is well-known in the field, I expected your appearance to be . . ."

"Normal?"

She frowns and shakes her head. "Not quite. Outlandish maybe? For starters, your clothes are pitch-black, belts hug your body, you're fairly thin, and your hair is worse than mine after I've woken up. Everything about you gives me unsettling vibes. It's almost like you're—"

"Death itself. Pardon me for my field of work. So many people come to me with terminal illnesses, and their sorrow damages my mentality and negatively stains my appearance. Sure, I can cure tragedies, but some of my clients are unsure how far gone they already are. Still, the medical field is always progressing, and unlike others, I will always strive to reverse a hopeless situation."

"So I've heard," she answers and attempts to peer over my shoulder.

"Would you like to come in?"

"I would appreciate that, thanks."

Her shoulders fall, and the spark in her eyes flickers. So, exhaustion finally claims its prize. I have her take my hand, her cold, fragile fingers wrapping against my own, and I lead her inside. She follows me to her chair. It's the same one my last patient met his end, and regardless of this fact, it's not bloody or imperfect in any way. After years of practice, I've perfected the art of treating my patients while not staining my furniture. My claws are to thank for that. Careful movements are its specialty. Entering a body and removing—

She withdraws her touch from mine as she sits. Getting comfortable, she rests an arm on the table next to her. I assume she might decide to lay her head down too, but her façade tells me she would never do such a thing, at least in front of me.

She looks at me with those emerald eyes, staying silent as if expecting me to push a conversation. I'm afraid of what she has come to tell me. Besides, I prefer to not dive into delicate situations immediately, so I leave her side and fill a glass of water. Even though it's from the same basin I wash my claws in, it's pure and fresh—as it should be when used to treat those blades. It's delicious too, and no sickness has befallen me for quite some time.

She takes the water from me and drinks it. After a few swallows, her skin seems to lose some color, and she closes her eyes longer than usual. Was the drink not satisfactory? She appears unwell.

"Thank you," she states, clearing her throat and placing the glass down next to her.

"So tell me," I begin as I sit opposite to her, "what

brings you here to see an old doctor like myself?"

She crosses her arms and stares me dead in the eyes, judgmental and suspicious. My instincts cause me to return her glare, and I do not waver.

"You're Rykar, correct?"

"I am."

"And you're the renowned doctor who will always attempt to cure the impossible?"

"Yes," I repeat. Why else would anyone come all this way?

"Well, I'm a doctor myself."

My eyes darken. Has she come all this way to criticize my work, or to uncover the whereabouts of those I failed to save? Does she plan to report her findings to Gresiden officials and have me arrested? What does she gain from my capture? Obviously less competition. I should have known from the start. Everyone who enters my home causes misery and anxiety, leaving me with a nasty headache to deal with.

"Since I am a doctor," she continues regardless of my warning glare, "I realize what I hope isn't true. I believe I'm deathly sick. Something isn't right with my heart. I'm hoping you can re-diagnose me and cure my ailment."

Taken aback, my heart aches from my lack of trust in her, a mistake I will not make again for one as beautiful as a blooming rose. But why her? Is she truly so far gone, and I just fail to see it? I refuse to believe such a thing, especially since I've never met another soul who shares my profession. Imagine all the stories and secrets and dark realities we could get off our chests.

But no. This is why I never pursued a relationship with another. Her past is likely filled with light dissipating the shadows. Mine was spent all alone, and despite the unimaginative start my parents gifted me, I've learned everything through practice, reading, and endless failures. Nobody will understand my passion when I fail to save others. They will always side with the dead, believing what I do is wrong. But what if she is different? She understands our role as saviors, so she should see my actions as justified. Besides, my hands are and shall always be clean.

So, I ask, "What is this ailment you have diagnosed upon yourself exactly? Most others who come to me appear on the verge of death, but you don't replicate that description. So, what is wrong?"

"Actually, I need to know if I can trust you, so you will answer your own question. And if you misdiagnose me, I might as well experience the rest of my days. Being on a countdown is a preferable scenario over being killed by a false doctor."

"Fair enough." I guess it's impossible to snuff out the negative theories and suspicions against me. My name will always raise doubt in the minds of others. It's tiring, and

the swelling hatred it entices frightens me.
Still, just for her, I will play her game.

She claims the problem lies with her heart, but I'm not one to jump to conclusions, at least not with her. If she is truly on the verge of death, I wish to believe she is healthy until the truth is inevitable. Therefore, I'll simply build a diagnosis based on all other symptoms, examining her heart last.

Looking at her face, my eyes instantly lock-on to her eyes—those unwavering, entrancing green eyes. Some say they are the window to the soul, and from what I see, there is hopelessness and a tinge of fear. Does she truly believe she is so far gone, or is the lack of faith in my abilities causing her to be afraid? There's no reason for those thoughts, because no matter what you think, I am no false doctor.

I push those thoughts away and drop to my knees so my eyes are level with hers. If she is in some sort of distress, I do not wish for her to stand or move. Each body part is a piece to a larger puzzle. When I manipulate each unperturbed section, I can then discover the source of what ails a human.

"You sure take a while to begin your examination," Isabelle judges harshly.

"Little do you know, I've already begun. Are other doctors so hasty to lay their hands on their patients?"

"Well, it would be a welcome change. Besides, some say touch is the first step toward understanding one another." She bats her eyes a few times and offers me a brief smile.

Blood rushes to my cheeks until I tear away my gaze from hers, instead shifting my focus to her bare legs. Why would a woman like her flirt with someone like me? How can she be so desperate? Perhaps she's as sick as she claims.

Following her desires, I apply mild pressure as I brush my hands across the skin of her knees. Afterward, I slide them down toward her ankles, letting the friction of our skin determine if anything is amiss.

There is almost no give; her legs are stiff and swollen.

"Can you feel my hands?" I ask.

"Barely. Can you squeeze them for me?"

She is definitely flirting, or offering me a hint. Still, her suggestion was unnecessary, for I was just asking a simple question before moving on.

I proceed to squeeze her calves, and the moment I do so, she rockets her head toward the sky, gritting her teeth.

Painful. Her eyes close, and her brows furrow, and her mouth contorts in strange ways as I shift my hands onto various sections of her legs and apply pressure. My hands become a little cramped after the fourth attempt to get a reaction out of her, but needless to say, she sat well. Perhaps now she won't tell me what to do, and I doubt she will blame me for the torture. This is what she wanted.

Looking up at her dulling eyes, a simply say, "Swollen legs."

She nods, confirming my suspicions.

"How long have you had them?"

She sighs deeply and answers, "Long enough. Maybe a few weeks? Sometimes the swelling goes down, but they're usually like this now."

Grimacing, I walk across the hardwood on my knees to get behind her.

"Breathe deep for me." She nods like she understands my command, but continues her standard rhythm. I raise an eyebrow as I wait for her to comply. Eventually, she begins to extend her inhale.

She coughs and hacks like she is choking on water. I'm afraid her lungs will leave her body if she doesn't stop. I embrace her from behind and rub her neck and chest, attempting to soothe her panicking, contorting body. This isn't the sort of cough warranted from choking, instead, the body is rejecting outside air due to a damaged passageway. She must calm herself, or her body will suffer further negative consequences from the inside.

Her flailing movements begin to slow, and it's clear she's trying to stabilize her breathing. Another coughing fit counteracts her efforts, so I squeeze tighter and stroke her neck some more. She calms down further, capturing multiple shallow breaths where she can. The coughing stops. She continues to breathe in rapid succession, and only then is her body stable once more. She's going to be okay.

"It's like what I told you, the power of touch is strong," she dares to mock me. However, when she looks at me, her eyes are watery and overflowing with misery.

"Isabelle, seeing you like this hurts more than you know. I wish I could alleviate your pain with a snap of the finger."

She nods, indicating for me to continue.

I reach for her hand, and she gives me it with her palm upward. Feeling her skin, it is soft and, unlike her legs, seemingly healthy. I apply pressure on her wrists, sensing her veins struggle to pump blood. It appears her heart rate is fairly standard, but her pulse and blood pressure are irregular. A veil of dread suffocates my heart as I suspect her diagnosis.

I frown. This woman needs to be okay. She appears fine from the outside! She walked here without any help!

She is the first real doctor I've ever met. Do not tell me she is fated to die. My claws will become tainted and will forever weigh me down.

Resting my head on her back, I only take a moment to listen to her heart and lungs coexisting and struggling in unison. This woman should not be alive right now. Her plight is as clear as rainwater.

This woman is walking death, as much as I hate to admit it. There is no way I can save her, but what if there is a solution? What if I lock myself in my study and look over all my books and notes and . . . do what I can? It's what I've always done. Nobody else will attempt such a thing. She will die either way. If I fail, I will not allow another to steal your heart. It will be mine to keep: a daunting reminder of my failure, a loving memory of your presence.

As I use the chair to help me to my feet, I turn my head away from her sorrowful eyes, which stare at my shoes. There is no use pretending everything is okay. The least I can do is tell her the truth.

"Heart failure," my voice cracks into a whisper.

"Good," she responds to her death sentence. "My life is in your hands, Doctor Rykar. I doubt I will live past this week, so I'm yours to do as you please. Just . . . try not to give up on me."

This is too much. This room is too stuffy. The smell of death overwhelms my nose and refuses to leave. So many people have died in this house, and yet, her ending is not something I wish to comply with. There must be an easy solution, but I know there isn't one.

I take a few deep breaths and leave. Why must it be my job to save people from their torturous fate? No matter, I will remove her curse one way or another. I just need some time alone in my office.

"Feel free to roam and make yourself comfortable," I remark with a fake smile over my shoulder. If she is smart and wishes to do something beneficial for the two of us, she shall leave before I commit to a regretful choice.

I shut the door behind me, mindful of the tension within my trembling arms. Next, I close the window's shutters, blackening my office enough to comfort myself and contemplate. This should be an easy choice to make.

The claws resting on my table watch me like a snake—entrancing—seemingly grinning at my agony. It knows what I must do. It knows that any other human in her position would already be witnessing their wrath. But her . . . she is different.

Returning to the water basin, I scrub my face raw with water, giving extra attention to my eyes. I'm seeing things. The claws shouldn't have a mind of their own. I control those beautiful weapons.

I continue to rub my eyes until they are dry. When I open them, the darkness paints a vivid picture of a man staring back at me. Tired, lonely, stale. His dead eyes beg me to do what must be done. As I consider his proposal, a smile forms on his face. He understands the need. He understands the desire. He understands what's best.

Shaking my head, I notice a few strands of hair out of place, destroying my appearance. So, I brush some cold water through my scalp, correcting the deviation and soothing my aching head. Furthermore, this is no time to look like a freak. I am sophisticated. I am a doctor. Healing people is what I do.

My eyes dart to the flowers on my desk. They may lead to some sort of solution. Even though they are the only medicines I use apart from surgery, their medicinal properties can cure a wide variety of poisons disrupting the body. Some can force someone into delirium while they aggressively heal, others can simply modify the consciousness of an individual. They have never driven me wrong before, and when they cannot cure, my decision is made.

Still, my eyes continue to divert from those radiant flowers and onto the blinding light of my claws. Unlike a painful, tedious process, these will guarantee to ease her suffering. Immediately.

I jerk my head away from their allure and stare at myself once more. My image shifts from a man to a woman, then back to my unsightly stature, then back to her angelic form. Isabelle. Our eyes are the same—green. Our professions and what we seek in the world are identical at heart. Together, we are both dying, only wishing to cure ourselves and others. Where you are young with an illness meant for a dying man in his eighties, I am a creature who is mentally ill from all the stress and burdens others have placed upon me. Even your burden hinders me, but still . . . you come to me seeking aid, and it's my duty to assist you.

Ah, but look who's come to assist me: divine judgment, a strange blackness manifesting next to my claws and watching me with its nothing eyes. A relic of my past. For many months now, it arrives and offers its wisdom, guiding me toward my final decision. The uncanny shadow averts its gaze to my desk and toward my claws. Is this really the right choice, shadow? Will this be my choice? What are you really?

I spin around to catch the shadow off guard. However, nothing is there. What did I expect? This shadow is me, the chaos that guides me.

My feet lead me toward the table, and soon, I'm standing where the darkness once stood. Here, a choice is presented to me: either I attempt to cure with medicine, waste precious time researching, or simply end her life for another's benefit. I can only imagine what discoveries can be made through examining her broken heart. Is it possible my buyers will develop a cure for the next person with heart failure? But what about her? What about now? Do I truly lack the skill to save her myself? She needs my help! I cannot give up on her!

I slam my fists on the table and recoil as pain sears in one of my hands. I inhale saliva and begin to cough. Some books fall, and the flowers in their vases shatter on the floor. It appears two of my fingers are bleeding heavily, so I grasp them tightly while coughing out my lungs, and only when I hear knocking on my door do I succeed in regaining some control over my respiratory system.

Isabelle breaks into my office and panics as she sees my claws, but unlike those before her, she dashes to me and takes my bare hand into hers, clenching onto my bleeding fingers. Fascinating.

"What happened? Are you okay?" her voice trembles as she stares at the blood seeping from my fingers onto hers. She shouldn't care this much, for the blades simply punished me for all the sorrow I have caused. It was only a matter of time.

"Wait right here!" she commands, guiding my other hand into a firm grip around my wound before running away. In mere seconds, she returns with her bag, setting it down on the table next to me. She digs through it and reveals some bandages, preparing them and constricting my two fingers with their fabric.

She works with incredible speed, her dedication and skill revealing how much talent this doctor possesses. Imagine if we combined our skills to ease this world's suffering.

"Those claws . . ." she says with wonder and a hint of concern. "You cut yourself."

I blink a few times, then usher her out of my office with my newly bandaged hand. "I just dropped something, that is all."

After we enter the living room, I slam the door behind me. She must not know about their use. My internal struggle is not hers to bear.

She smiles and sweetly says, "Are they used to defend yourself? Out here in the middle of nowhere, I guess you never know when someone wishes to break in and steal from a renowned doctor like yourself." A test, again.

"Sure, they could be used that way, but hopefully I never have to. But no, those claws are meant to carefully obtain flower parts to treat ailments. I'd rather not get my hands dirty and impurify their potency."

"Fair enough, but now you must wash them before you can reuse them. Nobody wants blood in their medicine festering away at the quality."

"I'll clean them. In fact, would you like to join me in some flower picking?" I hope this will divert her attention to something less serious.

"Does this mean you found a cure for me?" she falsely observes, her skin and eyes brightening with foolish joy.

"Still considering my options. So, what do you say?"

"I would love to!" she wastes no time responding. This forces a smile out of me. Her livelihood is remarkable, even if she's ignorant of the dark veil ticking down her time. How

I wish to keep her . . . and perhaps her light is what I need, the one who could help me defy my shadow. Besides, who's to say I can't find a cure? I can at least try.

Raising one finger from my damaged hand, I gesture for her to wait as I enter my office. She nods in compliance, and I leave her alone in the living room.

My eyes lock onto the claws, and I reach for them without hesitation. For the first time in my life, these weapons will not kill another who is deemed untreatable. Instead, Isabelle shall be the first visitor to witness their abilities and live to tell the tale.

Using the water basin in my office, I remove the blood from the few blades that licked my skin. I'd prefer to clean them where Isabelle waits, but I do not wish to scare her. Instead, I desire her first impression of me wielding claws to be one full of curiosity and awe. Let me redefine what these weapons represent, and let that be the first step toward change.

After the remaining blood is wiped away, I chance a look in the mirror. My face appears as a younger man full of hope, a hope like Isabelle's. I need to defy the odds just this one time. There is always a chance of success. Even my shadow agrees, for it no longer lingers behind my reflection, a welcome sight to behold.

Isabelle will be my greatest project yet.

The moment Isabelle and I step outside, the crisp air latches onto my lungs. It's great to finally leave, for the house was getting stuffy.

Additionally, with the cool temperature and the sun beaming down on us, my head feels lighter and my chest fluttery. Euphoria at its finest. This high will push me in the right direction. But first . . .

"So, where are you from exactly?" I inquire before heading to the back. The flowers can wait a moment longer.

"Lakrestram," she answers, enthusiastic in her response. "Have you ever been there?"

"I haven't."

"Hmmm. Where did you live before here? Surely you haven't lived all alone in this musty old place your entire life."

"Fair observation, but I might as well should have. No, I lived here since I was young, however, there was a time I resided in Gresiden's main kingdom. Living there was okay, and I did make some friends, but then my family was afraid of . . ."

"Afraid of what?" she asks quizzically, moving her head to my knees so I lock eyes with her. She is definitely a strange woman.

"I'm not sure." I shake my head, knowing I've revealed too much already. "Either way, we stayed here, they eventually grew old and sick, and I was left alone to study."

"Were they doctors, too?"

I release a small growl and answer, "Yes, but not quite as talented as me. Nonetheless, if it wasn't for their expertise, I would have never become successful or even meet you."

Still, maybe it would've been better if they weren't doctors. They ran from the law and started experimenting with the darker sides of medicine. From their legacy, I learned what I could and read their books, but where they were afraid to end someone's life for the advancement of the medical field, I was not. Our job as doctors has and always will be to achieve what's possible, learn from mistakes, then persevere. Perhaps once I cure her, she will understand. Though my path may seem evil to others, there is nothing I won't do for the good of the world.

I hear a gasp of pleasure from behind, only to find that she's snuck to the back of my house. I shake my head and follow her sound, and when I approach her, I can't help but mimic her delightful smile as she appreciates my garden—a vast variety of flowers and bushes used in medicine. Still, is this really something to be so excited about?

"You told me you've never seen thieves! This place is a doctor's dream!"

She dashes toward the flowers. "No thieves, only rabbits."

To confirm there hasn't been any intruders, I scan the fence line surrounding the garden. No holes. It doesn't matter too much anyway, since I suspect anything that eats these plants will suffer dire consequences.

"I can imagine all the money you saved by growing this yourself!" She can't be talking about those small bushes.

Raising an eyebrow, I question, "You spent money on pollux? Those exist in the wild."

"Not quite where I'm from. It's a sought-after sleep remedy, so vendors make it impossible to obtain for free, taking advantage of doctors."

"I see," I simply say. I did not know other kingdoms were so cruel. "Can you tell me what Lakrestram's like?"

"Colder than here." Isabelle moves away from the pollux and looks at some windrake flowers. "Like you, I live sort of far from the capital, but my home isn't as barren as yours. There's a beautiful loch where I love to go swimming. The water is clear, making it easy to see all the colorful fish. In the winter, it's fun to go out and run across the water, sliding and spinning. In fact, it should be that time of year in another month or so." Her eyes glisten with tears. She believes she will never return.

"Do you live with anyone?" I ask as she investigates some tylotus flowers, their long stems and colorful blooms standing out among the rest of the garden.

"No, just me."

"So, you really are like me," I say under my breath. She then stares at me, and I turn away. My heart races. She wasn't supposed to hear those words.

"You could say that," she responds to my thoughts. "Maybe it just means I placed my trust with the right person."

I release a small chuckle. "You're going to make me need some tylotus." Her smile disappears, obviously confused, so I quickly elaborate, "Tylotus cures congestion. Your words are too sweet, clogging my heart until it needs medical attention. Actually, you know what, never mind. I never make jokes anyway."

She laughs at my confusion and nods upward, inviting me to close the gap between us.

"You should make jokes more often, Rykar. The punchline is when you explain yourself. Go ahead and take one in case you need it. Let's see what those claws can do."

Nodding, I place one hand on the stem, then slice it free with the other. Seamless, sharp, no flesh.

"Even though that solves your problem, it doesn't solve

mine," her voice becomes bleak.

Refusing to look at her, I inspect the orange, whites, and greens of this particular flower in my hand and simply mutter, "I'm still working on a plan, assessing my options." I scan my garden for anything that could solve her predicament, or even something capable of prolonging her life. Ghost's whisper: a flower with white petals across the length of the stem. Dangerous. Can numb any pain but can destroy someone's mind with fictitious voices.

"I doubt ghost's whispers will help my case, Rykar," Isabelle says, even more distraught.

Grimacing, I consider the large red-petaled plant with thorns, mitsnapper. It can dissolve any burden within the body, but the potency could kill someone in minutes. Furthermore, I've only witnessed one successful case with it, but I failed to diagnose the survivor. As for its potential to reverse heart failure . . .

"Just admit it," her voice rings into my thoughts and makes me sick, "there's no cure for me."

I drop the tylotus flower and place my claws next to it. I then grab her freezing hands—soft as snow—and attempt to warm them in mine. "That's not true," I reassure, "I just need a bit more time." She knows I'm lying. There is no hope in her posture, only despair in her eyes. "What if we visit your home together when you're better?"

She takes a small breath and holds it. Did I surprise her

too much? Is she okay?

"Isabelle?"

"You'd want to go there? But what if someone else shows up when you're gone?"

I can't tell if she finds my idea distasteful, so I switch my stance. "There's nothing wrong with a vacation. Besides, I'm sick of my place and the same old scenery. Perhaps I wish to see the loch and go swimming with you. Maybe if I like it there, we can save lives together?"

If I fail, I'm setting myself up for disaster. If I kill her, my life would be marked with a death sentence—forever a doctor of misery.

She stares down at our feet and begins to cry, sniffling in an attempt to hold herself together. I'm afraid to push her further, so I just stand there, warming her hands in mine. What more can I do?

My eyes flicker when she looks up and smiles, her green eyes countering the bloodshot whites attempting to steal her beauty.

"In case it's all over for me soon, I'm okay waiting until tomorrow for any treatment," her voice quivers. "It would give you more time, and maybe you can comfort me for one final day before fate takes what it wants."

To comfort and spend extra time with her. I would come to know her, understand her, and see who she truly is despite our limited time. Perhaps this will influence my choice regarding her fate? After spending time in my garden, my hope is seemingly not as high as it once was. Therefore, I must prepare for the worst outcome; I need my fascination with her to dwindle. I still hope to save her, and I would love to visit Lakrestram, but this world is cold. We can't all have what we want. If I must kill her tomorrow, at least her organs will be fresh. Perhaps I can even find solace in believing another will examine her broken heart and formulate a cure.

"Very well," I answer as she watches me like I'm some sort of savior. "I will be there for you. We can live out a memorable night in case disaster befalls upon you. Upon us."

She pushes me and presents a massive smile, a genuine smile. "This doesn't mean you should skimp out on finding a cure."

"Don't worry, I'll be considering various options until tomorrow, even if it requires a restless night. Besides, I'm devising a plan as we speak."

"Mind if you share?"

I shake my head. "Not until I figure out the kinks, but you can trust me. Come tomorrow, your sickness will be no more."

Leaving the comfort of her hands, I grab my claws and the tylotus flower resting on the ground. An illusion of two choices. I don't spare her much of a glance as I get up, but when I walk, I know she is following me back inside. It's unfortunate I already know what I must do.

A chill runs across my spine as I feel a familiar presence indicating it is time. It will wait while I sleep, silent until I accept its invite. There is no use making it impatient. So, I carefully open my eyes, afraid to see what it wants, only to find Isabelle resting beside me. Her breathing is slow and even, obviously unattuned to the creature's craving. She reminds me of the dead: beautiful, preserved, unbothered by the living's presence as they stare and mourn. If only I could cure the incurable.

Spinning around, I move slow to prevent her from waking. Then I see it, the shadow watching me with its blank eyes, coaxing me to become entranced by it and become one. When it notices our connection, my shadow leaves through the closed door. You do want me to follow you, don't you? Is it time already?

The bed squeaks—loud enough to wake every soul

in Gresiden—as the pressure from my body gradually unburdens it. I continue to observe her peaceful rhythm as I stand, determining if she has awoken. She has not.

It is sad I will never see her like this again, alive without fear. You could've saved each of us the heartache if you just never came, but then I would've never met you. Maybe I won't give away all your organs. Your heart can stay with me.

I creep to the bedroom door and open it. Outside my bedroom, the moonlight shining through the windows cast long shadows in the darkness. This is his domain, for it only communicates when apart from the sun, and now it guides me toward this ultimate choice.

There is no sight of it anywhere, and it may be blending into the environment, but I don't require directions. I step out of the room and close the door, then head down the stairs and into my office. You never go anywhere else, shadow.

The moment I enter the room, faint whispering compels me to spin around and scan the blackness behind me. It might have been my imagination. I would've heard Isabelle follow me if she were here. Still, I will close the door just to be safe.

Once I hear the audible click, I survey the room and find nothing amiss. I see those claws waiting for me on the table, but first I must make myself presentable and check my mental state. I move to the mirror and stare back at my reflection. Here, I notice my hair is a bit off, so I cup some water from the basin. As I reach for my scalp, all the water splatters across my clothes. There is something in the mirror with me. My heart pounds harder, and my breathing hastens. I rub my eyes, quick and aggressive, but it stays.

My shadow now has a wicked smile—sharp, uneven teeth dwell within its mouth—reaching its eyes. Black horns protrude from its skull. Its outlandish, human-like shape coaxes me to appreciate its divinity.

"Hello?" I croak. The shadow stays and does nothing.

I spin away from the mirror and attempt to catch the creature off-guard, but I see nothing within the darkness. I shift my eyes back and forth to try and quell the anxiety overtaking my body. I inhale and exhale deep breaths. I relax my tense shoulders. All this is just punishment for what I must do. The world must be retaliating against me by sending such a vile creature. A demon, perhaps, or something far worse.

Nothing can stop me from what I must do, however. Those claws have never guided me in the wrong direction, and they won't ever do so.

The blades resting on my table shine bright with the moon's reflection. Where Isabelle is beautiful, so are these weapons. They share nothing alike, for one will age and die while the other stays loyal to me until the end of time, even when I'm buried.

"That woman is smarter than you think," the voice of fear incarnate speaks to me, causing every hair upon my body to stand on end. Strong hands clasp my shoulders and arms. Each finger pulls at my skin. Each claw tugs at my clothes as they scrape and catch.

I muster up all my courage and simply ask, "Who are you?"

"She knows you are going to kill her. She sits awake as we speak, awaiting her imminent demise for when you return," Death speaks to me. He needs no introduction, for there is nothing else this creature can be.

"Is it my time, Death?"

He releases a deep chuckle and swirls closer to face me head-on. My body refuses to move in his presence. If I disobey or do anything distasteful, he will kill me.

"Death? How amusing. For you, Rykar, this is perfect." I swallow hard, then the creature continues, "Dull, green eyes which have witnessed endless torture from countless emotions. You have experienced every beautiful sensation ranging from love and compassion to hatred and fear, sometimes all from the same humans. Ah, when you watched your patients extend their final breaths as you cut into them, I know you understood how they felt. It molds you into what you are today, an alluring bottle of chaos.

"Your posture also tells me you grew up under strict supervision. Is this perhaps you had the makings of a killer from such a young age? Could it have been you who killed those close to you?"

"I didn't kill anyone, especially not them," I retaliate.

"You wonder why your parents didn't live longer, Rykar? It's because you messed up. You gave them the wrong medicine when they specifically asked for another. Either you were incompetent or evil from the beginning."

"But I didn't—"

"But I like that about you," Death cuts me off, his acceptance allowing me to breathe easier. "You take chances. You weigh each person's life before passing judgment. You are not black and white."

"And why are you here? What does your presence mean for me?"

"It means I won't kill you. A demon like you could be very useful."

"Useful?" I wonder what this means for Isabelle. If I help Death, will I gain his favor? Could he prevent the unpreventable?

The creature before me transforms into a slender woman in a blink of an eye, blending well within the shadows. She walks toward me and cups my chin.

"Isabelle?"

She brushes her hand against my cheeks, calming me down. I breathe a sigh of relief and close my eyes with her touch. The moment I feel bliss, intense pressure encircles my neck as my head is jerked backward like she is about to slit my throat.

"Would you like to save me?" a feminine voice unlike Isabelle speaks.

"Yes."

"Would you like to let me live?"

"Yes."

"Even with sickness?"

Something sharp scratches against my neck. Warm blood runs down my chest.

"Only if you're cured," I whimper, and the sharp object leaves my throat. I regain a bit of confidence in my words as I add, "Curing you is the only way I'll let you live."

The wetness from my chest alleviates as my neck becomes sore. Is my blood retracting into my open wound? If Death is capable of this power . . .

As soon as the pain dissipates, she releases me, and I fall to my knees. I breathe deep in an attempt to calm down, but when I gaze upward toward Isabelle, I instead see myself standing before me, a full representation of my shadow. We lock eyes, and it stares deep into my soul. The longer we prolong our connection, the greater our understanding becomes.

"Rykar?" Someone knocks at the door. "Rykar, it's Isabelle. Is everything okay? Have you been eating ghost's whispers?"

She thinks I'm talking to myself. My shadow, Death, stares back at me, seemingly judging me for her intrusion on our conversation. I don't want her to be involved in this. She shouldn't have woken up. She should've stayed in bed and at least pretended to be asleep until I returned.

Death walks up to the door, and I dread what's to come.

"Everything is okay, Isabelle," he says to her with a voice close enough to mine. "I am perfecting your remedy, and it will be ready come tomorrow. I'll tell you everything then."

"Okay," she answers, devoid of emotion. She still assumes she's going to die. I hear her footsteps crawl back upstairs as I watch Death shapeshift into Isabelle's form once more. The creature smiles wide, unlike her, and it grabs my claws from the desk.

"What are you doing? Put those down."

The creature obliges and tosses them to me. They scatter across the floor, damaging every blade. When they eventually hit my feet, a wicked laugh resonates from Death's throat.

"Kill me, Rykar."

"What?"

"Kill me. Murder me without ill intent. Make my life useful by extracting my organs."

I shake my head, tears welling up in my eyes as I struggle to slip my hands into the claws. Why does she wish to accept this disastrous fate? Why does she beg for death instead of hope?

She moves closer to me and glares at my weak body.

"Get up and kill me, Rykar. Are you weak? I said stand!"

I finish arming myself and follow her command. My legs shake and threaten to give out, but I muster the strength to rise before her figure. I squint to force the tears out of my eyes and observe her beguiling body.

"Why make this difficult for me?" I plead, begging her to stop.

She seizes my hand and places it on her shadowy chest. "Just do it. Clench your fist and finish the job so I can stop torturing you. You wish to return to your bland life, don't you? A life without me?"

I can't do it. My hand slips away from Isabelle, and I fall back to the floor. Tears stream down my face as I succumb to this terrible emotion.

"You're weak," Death's voice speaks to me once more. "You have no other choice than to accept my gift: power to cure, strength of a god, potential to eradicate the death tormenting the walking dead. There will be no more concern of sickness for Isabelle's dying body, and she will stay vibrant. Trust me when I say she will not succumb to this heart failure."

I nod, and Death grabs my arm and lifts me to my feet. He then brushes my cheeks as his smile grows to an impossible size. I shut my eyes to remove any remaining tears, and upon opening them again, Death reinstates the shape of my shadow.

"Let us become one, Rykar."

Before I can question him, my body becomes numb as his shadowy mass steps into me. Within seconds, my body feels lighter, my sorrowful emotions disappear, and a rampant ache of immense power pounds against my insides wishing to break free. A smile manifests across my face.

I attempt to stretch in order to release the pent-up energy. However, my body refuses to obey. I squeeze my hand into a fist and scowl, or at least I try to, because even facial movements are rendered useless. My mind strains from the mental pressure I apply to even lift a finger. I must control this newfound vigor.

Against my volition, my mouth opens and declares, "Relax, Rykar, and enjoy the show. I will handle your beloved."

My body teleports to the room where Isabelle waits, and I see her sitting in a fetal position on my bed. She looks up at me and panics. I wish to comfort her and tell her there's nothing to be afraid of. Nonetheless, instead of waiting for Death to work his magic, she tries to flee. Half the blanket follows her frantic movements, and when I catch a glimpse of her eyes, a distressed fear clouds every part of their color. As she rushes by me to escape, my body snaps its fingers. She falls to the floor, limp as a three-day-old corpse.

What are you doing? Why did you kill her? I thought we had an agreement! I force my will against all the shadows hiding within my mind and soul. I must take back control! I push and push and internally scream. I need to comfort her! This is not what I wanted!

My efforts take effect as I regain control of my body. I run to her and hold her limp shell. My heart yearns for her to be alive. Her diminishing warmth tells me it's already too late. Why grant me hope only to steal it away?

"Satisfied?" Death asks over my shoulder.

"No, you killed her!" I yell at him. I need to kill him and make him suffer, but Isabelle needs me right now.

Death laughs. "I killed her? This was all you, your power."

"YOU LIE!" I drop Isabelle and slash at the shadowy figure. Before my blades can reach their mark, a heavy wave of fatigue overtakes me. My heart becomes heavy and weak. I collapse to the floor next to Isabelle. As my vision blurs, the residing warmth within her body comforts me, for it withholds a foreign sense of peace. Even if I can't defeat him, at least I can find some solace in dying together. In some sick way, you ended my endless torment.

The sunlight assaults my eyes and burns my vision. I can't see a thing with how bright it is, but I feel someone move next to me. My head aches, I feel woozy, and I feel sick. What is going on?

Using my hand to block out the raging sunlight, my eyes quickly adjust to my surroundings. I'm in a room, and unlike mine, the sheets are blue, and there are various decorations across the walls. This is not my home.

Isabelle takes a deep breath next to me. She's still asleep. Was everything just a dream? Could it be that I saved her and don't remember, and now we are together, traveling the world? Was Death just a terrible figment of my imagination?

"Rykar, I don't know how you did it, but I feel so much better," Isabelle slurs her words next to me as she wakes up. "You must be the first person to cure heart failure. Imagine all the lives you could save."

"Where are we?"

"My place, don't you remember? After you cured me, we traveled to Lakrestram to continue assessing my condition. In fact, can you check me over again? I still find it difficult to believe."

She sits up and taps the veins on her wrist, so I grab it and assess her blood pressure. There is nothing unusual. She is stable. I must know for certain. I must know if Isabelle is truly alive and well. Therefore, I listen to her heartbeat by placing an ear on her back and a hand on her chest.

As I attempt to listen to her renewed life, Death manifests from nothing and watches. He stands in a corner, right out of sight from Isabelle, smiling and nodding—seemingly encouraging me to continue. I don't wish to scare her, so I continue to listen until I can fully grasp her condition.

She is normal . . .

I back off from her. I can't believe it.

Isabelle looks at Death for a moment before returning her gaze back to mine. "Well?"

"Do you see him?" I whisper just loud enough for her to hear.

"See who?" She follows my gaze toward Death, but again she doesn't shudder in fear or anything! How can she be so brave?

"I don't see anything," she lies.

"What? You don't see . . ." Death takes a step back and

dissolves into the wall.

"I get you've been through a lot of stress recently. Maybe some time in the loch would do you some good? Swimming always clears my head, and the cold water should wake you right up!"

"Give me a moment, I need some fresh air," I respond before I lose my composure. Getting out of bed, I ignore her judgmental eyes watching my every movement as I leave the room. I then spot the front door and exit, ridding myself of the house's toxicity.

The crisp air extracts any grogginess left within me. Still, I cannot recall anything Isabelle told me. I would remember saving her. I would remember the trip. I . . . wouldn't misplace my claws.

As I stare at my bare hands, I know something isn't right. I saw her die before my eyes. If so, who is she?

I take a few deep breaths and whisper to the wind, "What I need are some answers. I don't need to take a swim. I know what I saw and none of this makes sense. So, what is—"

"Going on?" Death finishes my sentence.

He stands before me and takes on a more humanlike appearance. The direct sunlight hitting his skin doesn't quite change his shadowy form, but no longer does he hide within the darkness. Here, he doesn't appear so frightening.

Despite my lack of trust, he's the only one with answers, so I ask, "Was that all a dream? Can you explain what is going on?"

He places a hand on my shoulder as if offering his respect. However, this time he doesn't scrape my body with his claws or hold me captive.

"A reward for a job well done," he announces louder than I would've preferred. "Rykar, you saved her with your newfound power. All I did was teleport you two here. Was that not the plan?"

"I saw her die."

"You saw a lie."

Isabelle exits her house and exclaims, "There you are! I thought you would've wanted to go together." She still doesn't see him. It's possible he's just in my head, or my closeness with the creature allows only me to see him.

Death grins and fades into the ground. The moment he disappears, dark clouds blot out the sunlight, making it much colder than before.

"Maybe it's best if we don't swim today," I suggest.

"It is a bit cold, but we can at least walk along the shore?"

I nod, then look over at the distant kingdom, Lakrestram. "You must be lonely here."

"No longer as lonely with you, that is, if you decide to stay?"

Offering a half smile, I answer, "I would love nothing more." It's best I leave my old life behind. Perhaps it's time to focus on myself for a change and heal my mentality with her help.

She offers me a hand and I take it. Together, we walk to the shore of the loch and stare into the water. My reflection is misshapen, and my eyes . . . they are different. Where my pupils were once round, now they appear as slits, expressing my green eyes further.

"Do I look strange to you?" I ask her.

She turns to me and cocks her head, seemingly curious and misunderstanding. "You appear the same. Why do you ask?"

"Never mind." It must be the way my reflection appears, for it's not my mirror.

"So, what do you think of the water?" Isabelle's hand squeezes mine tighter. "It's beautiful, isn't it?"

I nod, examining and searching for all the positives I can say about the loch. Somehow it is clearer than I imagined. There is little I cannot see within its depths: small, colorful fish swim together, some larger fish travel independently, and large rocks rest at the loch's floor. Furthermore, the water within my home doesn't match its beautiful blue sheen. How much I would love to dive right in and explore it all. I wonder if I could reach the sand and rock at the bottom?

Intense pressure suddenly crushes my lungs. I can no longer breathe. I'm freezing. I'm drenched. My eyes sting, but I force them to stay open. Somehow, I seem to be deep within the loch.

Above me, the vague, wavering figure of Isabelle is moving in frantic bursts.

Death manifests before me. He shakes his head and frowns, yet his eyes are bright and joyous.

"You have so much to learn," he says clearly despite being in the water. "Teleporting to the bottom of this loch? Rookie mistake. Still, I'm also learning from you, so your mistake can be forgiven. Despite all your trouble, I consider you a success."

He holds a finger to his mouth, smiling and baring his uneven teeth, then points up. A large splash of water captures my attention, and I see Isabelle swimming my way, fear clouding her eyes and her movements desperate.

Don't try to save me, I can get out of this mess! I leave Death's side and match Isabelle's movements, attempting to reach her. However, the burden upon my lungs deepens, and my muscles feel weak. There is no way I'm even getting close to her. I've wasted too much time listening to Death.

"Would you like some help?" He teleports in front of me and blows an air bubble. It expands and envelops my head, and I gasp for air, but I can't afford to stop moving. Isabelle's movements are slowing down. I'm running out of time!

Death chuckles from below. "You have the power of a demon, Rykar. Use it."

My movements hasten as I see Isabelle using the last of her energy for one final push. We are still far away from each other. I will never make it in time! What does Death even expect me to do!?

Her body expends the last of its energy, and I see her go limp in the water, floating in the infinite space.

"No!" I cry out.

"Use it," Death commands once more.

My mind is in disarray, and all I can think about is reaching her before she cannot be saved. I need to bring her to the surface; she needs to breathe. We need to get out of the water!

The gravity surrounding me seems to lessen momentarily as I find myself holding Isabelle within my arms.

"What is going—" The wet sensation surrounding us evaporates immediately, and Isabelle's sudden weight causes me to nearly drop her. I bring her to the ground— soft grass and dirt next to the loch—and immediately work toward making her heart beat once more. I don't know what happened or how we made it back on land so suddenly, but it doesn't matter. What matters is bringing her back to life. I know I can do it. She has only been unconscious for a brief moment.

I press my hands against her chest in perfect rhythm. After a moment, I breathe air into her lungs, then I apply more pressure against her chest.

Why hasn't she woken up yet? My motions become more desperate. The longer she doesn't return to life, the less chance of survival she has.

"Come on, Isabelle! Why did you jump in after me!? Please come back to—"

A heavy, blunt force smacks the side of my skull. I fall backward, and my entire head erupts in pain. As I look up, my vision is blurry and I feel nauseous. I blink a few times until I can interpret the harsh reality before me. Between Isabelle and I, the one who disrupted her revival, is Death, scowling.

"Demons cannot bring back the dead," he growls. "Even with magic, it is a pointless folly."

Before I can stand, Death grabs her limp body and throws it back into the loch with one singular movement.

"NO!" I scream and scramble and jump back in to save her. A sharp pain erupts from my leg as I'm flung back toward land, away from the water.

Death—now wielding my claws—shakes his head. He then removes and tosses me my weapons. I catch them and put them on. If he's going to stand in my way, then I'm left with no other choice. This time, I won't let him get away with this.

My leg sears in pain as I stand. Blood covers my foot and continues to seep out.

"Your power, Rykar, use it. Stop being weak and believe the impossible. Remember that night you came to me."

That night . . . I wrap a hand around my neck and rub

the smooth skin. I then shift my attention toward my bloody leg, imagining the muscles sewing themselves back together and the wound closing. Without warning, the familiar, unorthodox experience enwraps my leg. My blood returns to the wound, and within seconds, the injury is no more.

"You wish to kill me? Prove your determination." Death provokes, and I rush forward and swipe his face. He sidesteps just in time, so I shift and use both my hands to close in on his body. When my blades reach their mark, he evaporates in thin air.

"I promised her body would stay alive without illness," he speaks and claws my back. I cry out in pain and swipe backward, only for him to grab my arm and snap the joint. My arm goes limp. Agony and fear pulse through every inch of my body. He disappears again, and I attempt to heal my arm and back, an action which should be impossible, only for my suffering to lessen to soreness.

Grimacing and clenching my teeth, I apply every bit of concentration toward finding where he went. The moment he shows himself—

I project my once broken arm forward and grasp Death's face. Caught him. He looks surprised, but he doesn't struggle, so I let the metal claws close into his shadowy head as I swipe my other hand across his body. He makes no sound as his body bleeds and melts away until he's nothing but a black puddle of darkness.

"Isabelle!" I run toward the water again, only to feel something grip the back of my neck and lift me high into the sky.

It hurts. My hands attempt to cling onto the thing that holds me. It's difficult to breathe. My fingers eventually succeed in supporting my body, but the thing twists my neck to force me to look at it.

A large arm—at least thirty feet—extends from the black puddle. Then, seven more shadowy arms emerge from the darkness, each of identical height and girth. Two eyes . . . then four . . . eight green eyes stare at me as the creature's large mass completes itself. It bares its sharp fangs. It hisses and spews saliva across my body as it roars.

All the blood drains from my face. I scream, and the creature constricts my neck, making it difficult to produce any more sound. I cough and fight for air, striving not to pass out. Another hand pets my hair. It's wet and gross, yet cold and familiar. The creature smiles at my anguish.

"Isabelle is safe within the water," it gurgles. "I made a promise to you. Now she can rest and be vibrant here, and you can complete your debt without distraction."

I attempt to slice his arm, but the weapon ricochets off his skin. The attempt causes the monster to squeeze me tighter until I gasp for air. Panic rises, and I grasp and claw at his arm to support my body and beg him to stop. He complies and alleviates just enough pressure to postpone my death.

"Oh, poor Rykar, thought he could kill what he called Death. You cannot hurt me in my realm. Even if you ripped out my throat and sliced me into a million pieces, I would be unperturbed in the real world. You are also safe in this place, The Endless Abyss, a land of nothingness and infinite time."

Cold raindrops splatter across my face, forcing me to shut my eyes. After a few seconds, the rain softens into soft, freezing liquid. Snow. The sun then disappears across the horizon like it is being chased by a predator, and left in its wake is the full moon. The creature watches me within the darkness, its eyes glowing with glee.

"Still, it's fun to see your weak little eyes be afraid," it continues. "Transform that fear into something useful. You will have infinite time to learn and grow and become strong, and when you do, I will seek out your soul. Together, we shall savor newfound misery: a deep struggle unlike anything ever witnessed upon this planet."

The creature swallows me whole before I can consider its final words, and I awake back at home in my bed: unscathed, alone, emptiness clouding my heart.

My vision flickers, and I notice something watching me in the corner. I rub my eyes and look again, but there is nothing there. It must've been my imagination.

I stand and stare out my window. The sun's rays beam down just like yesterday, but this time, there is no Isabelle. There are no beautiful, emerald eyes to enjoy. There is nothing to look forward to. She is gone, stolen away from me. Does anybody really need me anymore? What happens if I simply disappear?

"Do not worry," Death speaks to me from everywhere and nowhere. "I need you, and you're mine for the rest of time. Nobody else is worthy of you. So please, explore the world. Demonstrate what your suffering can amount to." His voice fades away as he laughs, and I am left alone.

Frowning, I hold my bloody claws to my chest and let the blades scrape against me as I hug myself. This was all my fault, not Death's. He guided me toward a path I wasn't strong enough to follow. If I was not weak, I could have saved her with his gift. She would have lived, and there would have been no reason to suffer like so.

Instead, the creature's worst crime was giving me hope. I accepted her death already, and you came by and gave me a chance to save her. Then I failed. So now, I will close my heart and become stronger to uphold my end of the bargain. I will follow your wisdom and unlock my potential as a demon.

Zaven Boswell is an Iowa author who studied at Des Moines Area Community College and Iowa State University with a focus on creative writing. After becoming inspired by the great fictional stories that exist in today's media, he strives to create dark stories with an incentive on emotion—tales which allow readers to immerse themselves within the overall plot. In his pastime, he enjoys reading and watching movies with his fiancé and cat, as well as playing video games such as *Kingdom Hearts* and *Final Fantasy*.

Twitter: @FeignedShadows
Instagram: @feignedshadows

www.ingramcontent.com/pod-product-compliance
Lightning Source LLC
Chambersburg PA
CBHW030959310726
48969CB00008B/2401